P9-CED-666

THE UGLY DUCKLING

WRITTEN BY
HANS CHRISTIAN ANDERSEN

RETOLD AND ILLUSTRATED BY
RACHEL ISADORA

G. P. PUTNAM'S SONS

Once upon a time, at an old farm,
a mother duck sat on her eggs. One by one,
the shells began to crack, and out came
six chirping ducklings. "Peep, peep."

But the biggest egg still did not hatch.
"I will sit on it awhile longer," said
the mother duck.

When the egg finally hatched,
out came a strange-looking duckling
who gazed up at his worried mother.
"He is my child, but not at all like
the others," she said.

No one wanted to play with the poor ugly duckling. He was large and clumsy and so different from his brothers and sisters. All the animals on the farm laughed at him and teased him.

At night the ugly duckling
would cry himself to sleep.

One day, the duckling felt he had no choice but to fly away.
He came to a pond where some wild ducks lived.

"Do you know of any ducklings with gray feathers like me?" he asked.

"No," they all said. "We don't know any ducklings as ugly as you."

The duckling then came upon a pair of geese, who warned him not to stay at the pond. "It's dangerous here! There are men and dogs hunting!"

Just then, *pop! pop!* sounded
in the air, and two geese fell
from the sky.

The frightened duckling tried to hide. But a large dog ran up to him. The dog's jaws were open, showing his sharp teeth. But just as suddenly, the dog went on his way without touching the ugly duckling.

Oh, thought the duckling, *now I am thankful I am so ugly, even a dog will not bite me.*

When the hunters were gone, the duckling ran off.
A storm was blowing, so he sneaked inside a hut.
Here he found an old woman with her beloved cat
and hen. "What a prize!" the woman said
when she spotted the duckling.
"Now I shall have some duck eggs."

But after many weeks, there were
no eggs. "Well, you can't lay eggs
like me," said Hen. "Can you
purr like Cat?"

"No," said the duckling,
"but I like to swim and dive."
The hen and cat laughed at
his foolishness.

They don't understand me either, thought the duckling. "I think I will go back out into the world," he told them.

"Yes!" said Hen. "Do go."

Back at the pond, the duckling would swim and dive each day. Still, no creatures would come near him. One fall evening he saw a flock of the most beautiful birds.

He was filled with longing. "If only I could be as lovely as they!" the ugly duckling sighed.

Winter came and the land was covered with snow and ice. One day, as the poor duckling tried to find food, he dropped, exhausted, to the ground.

A kind farmer came upon him. "I'll take him home so that my children can look after him. Poor thing, he's frozen!"

The duckling was showered with kindness,
and in this way he survived the cold winter.

By the time spring arrived, the
duckling had grown so large that
the farmer set him free on the pond.
That is when the duckling saw himself
mirrored in the water.

"Goodness! How I have changed!
I don't recognize myself at all!"

At that moment, the beautiful birds he had seen before glided onto the pond. When the duckling saw them, he realized he was one of them. They surrounded him and stroked his long neck with their beaks as a welcome. Some children came to see the birds, and one of them exclaimed, "Look at the new swan! He is the most beautiful of all!"

At first, the young swan was shy and could not believe his good fortune. "I never dreamed of such happiness as this when I was an ugly duckling," he said to himself.

Then the young swan rustled his feathers, curved his long slender neck, and glided on the water into the bright sunlight.

For Nicholas

G. P. PUTNAM'S SONS

A division of Penguin Young Readers Group. Published by The Penguin Group.

Penguin Group (USA) Inc., 375 Hudson Street, New York, NY 10014, U.S.A.

Penguin Group (Canada), 90 Eglinton Avenue East, Suite 700, Toronto, Ontario M4P 2Y3, Canada (a division of Pearson Penguin Canada Inc.).

Penguin Books Ltd, 80 Strand, London WC2R 0RL, England.

Penguin Ireland, 25 St. Stephen's Green, Dublin 2, Ireland (a division of Penguin Books Ltd.).

Penguin Group (Australia), 250 Camberwell Road, Camberwell, Victoria 3124, Australia (a division of Pearson Australia Group Pty Ltd).

Penguin Books India Pvt Ltd, 11 Community Centre, Panchsheel Park, New Delhi - 110 017, India.

Penguin Group (NZ), 67 Apollo Drive, Rosedale, North Shore 0632, New Zealand (a division of Pearson New Zealand Ltd).

Penguin Books (South Africa) (Pty) Ltd, 24 Sturdee Avenue, Rosebank, Johannesburg 2196, South Africa.

Penguin Books Ltd, Registered Offices: 80 Strand, London WC2R 0RL, England.

Published simultaneously in Canada. Manufactured in China by South China Printing Co. Ltd.

Design by Marikka Tamura. Text set in Geist.

The illustrations were done with oil paints, printed paper and palette paper.

Library of Congress Cataloging-in-Publication Data available upon request.

Isadora, Rachel. The ugly duckling / by Hans Christian Andersen ; retold and illustrated by Rachel Isadora.   p. cm.

Summary: In this retelling of the Ugly Duckling, set on the African continent, the duckling spends an unhappy year ostracized by

the other animals before he grows into a beautiful swan.

[1. Fairy tales.] I. Andersen, H. C. (Hans Christian), 1805–1875. Grimme ælling. English. II. Title.

PZ8.I84Ug 2009   [E]—dc22   2008036514

ISBN 978-0-399-25029-3

3 5 7 9 10 8 6 4